THE MYSTERY AT CAPE COD

MAIN LIBRARY
Champaign Public Library
200 West Green Street
Champaign, Illinois 61820-5193

Copyright ©2010 Carole Marsh/Gallopade International/Peachtree City, GA
All rights reserved.
First Edition

Carole Marsh Mysteries™ and its skull colophon are the property of Carole Marsh and Gallopade International.

Published by Gallopade International/Carole Marsh Books. Printed in the United States of America.

Editor: Janice Baker
Assistant Editor: Sherri Smith Brown
Cover Design: Vicki DeJoy
Content Design: Randolyn Friedlander

Gallopade International is introducing SAT words that kids need to know in each new book that we publish. The SAT words are bold in the story. Look for this special logo beside each word in the glossary. Happy Learning!

Gallopade is proud to be a member and supporter of these educational organizations and associations:

American Booksellers Association
American Library Association
International Reading Association
National Association for Gifted Children
The National School Supply and Equipment Association
The National Council for the Social Studies
Museum Store Association
Association of Partners for Public Lands
Association of Booksellers for Children
Association for the Study of African American Life and History
National Alliance of Black School Educators

This book is a complete work of fiction. All events are fictionalized, and although the names of real people are used, their characterization in this book is fiction. All attractions, product names, or other works mentioned in this book are trademarks of their respective owners and the names and images used in this book are strictly for editorial purposes; no commercial claims to their use is claimed by the author or publisher.

Without limiting the rights under copyright reserved above, no part of this publication may be reproduced, stored in or introduced into a retrieval system, or transmitted, in any form or by any means (electronic, mechanical, photocopying, recording or otherwise), without the prior written permission of both the copyright owner and the above publisher of this book.

The scanning, uploading, and distribution of this book via the Internet or via any other means without the permission of the publisher is illegal and punishable by law. Please purchase only authorized electronic editions and do not participate in or encourage electronic piracy of copyrightable materials. Your support of the author's rights is appreciated.

Once upon a time...

Papa said …

Why don't you set the stories in real locations?

That's a great idea! And if I do that, I might as well choose real kids as characters in the stories! But which kids would I pick?

MiMi, PiCK ME, PiCK ME!

ME, TOO, MiMi, PiCK ME, TOO!

Christina

Grant

Pick me!

You two really are characters, that's all I've got to say!

Yes you are! And, of course I choose you! But what should I write about?

 National Parks!

 **SCARY PLACES!**

Famous Places!

FUN PLACES!

Disney World!

New York City!

Dracula's Castle

GRAND CANYON

On the *Mystery Girl* airplane ...

I CAN FLY US ANYWHERE!

Mystery Girl

Or aboard the *Mimi*!

Mimi

Take me to the Forbidden City!

Or by surfboard, rickshaw, motorbike, camel ...

All great ideas! I can put a lot of history, MYSTERY, legend, lore, and laughs in the books! We can use other boys and girls in the books. It will be educational and fun!

Good stuff!

Where will you get the other kids, Mimi?

From my Fan Club! Kids can apply to be characters!

Fan Club

And can you put some cool stuff online? Like a Book Club and a Scavenger Hunt and a Map so we can track our adventures?

Of course!

And can cousins Avery and Ella and Evan and some of our friends be in the books?

Of course!

Can I apply?

LET'S GO!

$\mathcal{A}$nd so, Mimi, Papa, Christina, and Grant took off aboard the *Mystery Girl* and America's National Mystery Book Series—where the adventure is real and so are the characters! —was born.

START YOUR ADVENTURE TODAY!

1
WHAT'S A CAPE COD?

"Wake up," yelled Grant, shaking Christina's arm. "Papa says there's Cape Cod!"

Christina's blue eyes flew open just as Papa dipped the left wing of his little red and white airplane, the *Mystery Girl*. She peered out the window. Her stick-straight brown hair danced around her shoulders. She was excited! Below was the sparkling white coastline of Cape Cod, their vacation destination.

"I don't get it," said Grant, disappointment in his voice. "I don't see a cape, and I don't see a cod."

"Actually, Cape Cod is a peninsula," said Mimi, closing her guidebook.

"What's a pen-soo-la?" asked Grant.

"A peninsula," said Mimi, emphasizing the correct pronunciation of the word, "is a piece of land almost surrounded by water. Cape Cod juts out into the Atlantic Ocean. See?" As Mimi pointed out the window, a cluster of sparkly red bracelets jangled on her wrist.

Mimi read a few lines from her guidebook about how great glaciers formed Cape Cod thousands and thousands of years ago. "See those cliffs down there near the coast line?" she asked. "They were shaped by the glaciers."

"Wow!" said Grant. "You mean ice moved across the land and pushed up all those rocks and sand down there into the ocean to make Cape Cod?"

"That's right," said Mimi.

"You know, your grandma spent a lot of time in Cape Cod when she was younger," said Papa, pushing back his black cowboy hat. He patted Mimi's hand. "That was before I knew her."

"Yes," said Mimi. "I had just graduated from college. Some girlfriends and I came to Cape Cod because we wanted to write. We joined a group of writers living near the town of Truro. We thought it sounded romantic."

"What was Cape Cod like back then?" asked Christina.

"A lot like it is now," said Mimi. "100-foot sand dunes. Windswept marshes. Wild, pink beach roses growing in the sand. Weathered houses, windmills, and lighthouses. Of course, the Cape is a lot more crowded now, especially Provincetown." Mimi sighed.

"Did you write a mystery book while you were there, Mimi?" asked Christina. She was proud that her grandma was Carole Marsh, the famous writer of children's mysteries. Papa flew the *Mystery Girl* all over the world so Mimi could do research for her novels. Christina and Grant traveled with their grandparents whenever they could.

"No, I just thought about it," replied Mimi, winking.

"What's all that red stuff down there?" asked Grant with his nose plastered against the plane's window. "It looks like a huge bowl of cherries."

"Those must be the cranberry bogs," said Papa. "It's more like a huge bowl of cranberries. It's October so cranberries are being harvested right now on Cape Cod."

"Can you tell that Cape Cod is shaped like a giant bent arm?" asked Mimi. "The town of Bourne is located at its shoulder. Eastham, where we are staying, is at the elbow. And Provincetown, where we are landing, is on the fist."

"It looks like a giant fishhook to me," Grant said. "That's it, it's a giant hook with a cod on it!" He giggled at his own joke. "Get it?"

Mimi and Papa smiled as Grant shoved his new iPod ear buds back into his ears. His eyes closed and his head of unruly blond hair swayed to the music.

"Did you know Cape Cod is where they transmitted the very first transatlantic wireless message?" Papa said loudly, glancing over his shoulder at Grant.

"What?" shouted Grant.

"First wireless message. Cape Cod!" Papa shouted back.

Grant gave a "thumbs up" and kept jiving. Papa's wireless message was definitely not getting through!

Christina rolled her eyes at her brother. "Are we going to Truro, Mimi?"

"Yes, Sweetie, I think we will stay with my old friend's daughter Arabella and her husband Ben at their cottage in Chatham for two nights. Then we'll go to Truro for a day. We'll have a nice, relaxing vacation—no researching. No mysteries for us!"

"You always say that," said Christina, teasing her blond, blue-eyed grandma, who was pulling her cherry red sweater up around her shoulders. Mimi smiled at Christina, her eyes twinkling.

Suddenly, Papa's radio blared.

"*Mystery Girl*, this is Provincetown Air Traffic Control. Weather conditions indicate that a nor'easter is developing off the coast of Maine. Its projected path includes the entire New England coast. Landfall may occur within 48 to 72 hours. This storm could bring precipitation, gale force winds, rough seas, and coastal flooding. Please divert your landing from Provincetown to Boston's Logan Airport!"

2
WHERE'S THE CAWD?

Mimi threw her arms around the tall, blond woman. "Oh, Arabella, you aren't a teenager anymore!" said Mimi and kissed Arabella's cheek.

"It's wonderful to see you, Mimi," said Arabella, hugging Mimi back.

Mimi introduced Arabella Cawthorne to everyone.

"Thank you for driving to Boston instead of Provincetown to pick us up," said Papa. "We couldn't land the *Mystery Girl* on the Cape with the storm heading this way."

"I'm happy to do it," said Arabella. "And here are two of your biggest fans, Mimi. Meet my neighbors, Amelia and Quincy Winthrop. They are just about Christina and Grant's ages. They have read all your books. They also know all about Christina and Grant's adventures!"

Christina instantly liked Amelia. She had curly, dark brown hair and sparkly blue eyes. Quincy looked very much like his older sister. Grant gave him a high-five that made them both giggle.

"Well, I know what I want to do first," said Papa. "I'm hungry. Let's chow down on some Boston seafood!"

"Some BAWSTON seafood," said Grant in his best Boston accent. "I want some BAWSTON CAWDFISH!"

Arabella maneuvered the car through heavy Boston traffic. Soon, the group was ordering lunch at the Legal Seafood Restaurant on bustling Long Wharf. From their table, they watched hundreds of ships going in and out of Boston Harbor.

"Look at that white, double-decker cruise boat leaving the pier," said Mimi. "Those people are headed out to watch for whales."

"Sometimes you can catch a glimpse of a whale from here!" said Arabella.

Immediately, all four kids leaned toward the windows to peer at the harbor.

"I can't see," said Grant, stretching on his tiptoes to peek over Christina's head. After a few minutes, he flopped back down in his chair. "There's not a single whale out there," he said, dejected.

Mimi saw their excitement and their disappointment. "Let's all go on a whale watch cruise," she said. "We can take one out of Provincetown or Barnstable. We might even go over to Nantucket. That's one of the great whaling seaports of the world."

"Yessss!" cried Grant. The other kids beamed with anticipation.

"There's the USS *Constitution*," said Amelia. She pointed toward an old, wooden ship with white billowing sails docked in the harbor.

"Is that the ship they call 'Old Ironsides'?" asked Christina.

"Yes," Amelia replied. "She is over 200 years old. President George Washington named her after the Constitution of the United States of America. My father and mother brought us up to Boston once on the Fourth of July. We watched her sail around the harbor!"

"Why do you call a ship a 'she'?" asked Quincy, looking puzzled.

"My father always said that it was because men love them!" answered Amelia. Everyone chuckled.

"You sure know a lot about ships," said Papa, who was as fascinated by them as he was by airplanes.

"Our father was a fisherman," said Amelia. "He died at sea during a terrible storm when I was seven years old. But I remember him taking me sailing. When I grow up, I want to do something with boats and the ocean."

"I think Amelia should take care of the lighthouse, like our mother," said Quincy.

Just then, three waiters arrived at their table. They balanced plates of steaming cod sticks, fried clams, lobster, and oysters.

"Wow, that's a lot of fish!" said Grant. He held up the codfish-shaped menu he was coloring and "swam" it around the table.

Quincy waved his menu like a swimming fish, too. "Now we have a school of codfish!" he said. The boys giggled.

"This is a lot of fish," said Arabella, dipping a chunk of lobster into glistening melted butter. "Of course, that's what this area is known for. Members of my husband's family have been Cape Cod fishermen since the mid-1800s."

"What's his catch?" asked Papa.

"Mostly codfish, which the Cape waters are famous for," said Arabella. "But there aren't as many cod as there used to be. Some fishermen have caught more than they should. That, plus boat problems have left Ben out of work lately."

"I'm sorry to hear that, Arabella," said Mimi.

"My teaching job helps, but it's not enough for boat repair," said Arabella, her green eyes looking sad. "There's a lady in town who wants to buy our cottage to turn it into a bed and breakfast inn. Ben says absolutely not, but sometimes I think we should. I can't imagine leaving Cape Cod, though."

"No, you can't leave," cried Quincy. "You're the best neighbors ever!"

With full stomachs, the group walked back to Arabella's car. As Grant scrambled into the back seat, Christina spied a piece of paper stuck to his shoe. "Stand still, Grant," she said, reaching down to pick it off.

"Isn't this a strange note?" asked Christina, then read it to the other three kids.

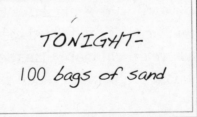

TONIGHT—
100 bags of sand

I wonder what it means, she thought, stuffing the note in the pocket of her blue fleece jacket.

"Speaking of sand, we need your help," whispered Amelia. "The sand dunes on Cape Cod are disappearing!"

3
ROCKS, BUZZARDS, AND SANDWICHES

Arabella turned the car south. Gradually, Boston's hustle and bustle gave way to the rural countryside of southern Massachusetts. "I have a treat to show you," Arabella remarked. "I know you all love history, so I'm taking you to one of the oldest historic sites in America!"

Christina was thrilled to see Arabella park the car next to a sign along the waterfront that said PLYMOUTH ROCK. She had just studied about the Pilgrims and Plymouth Rock in school!

The group walked over to a stately concrete monument with columns. In the center of the monument lay a smooth, odd-shaped rock.

"Here's where they say the Pilgrims landed," Arabella said. She pointed to the famous rock with 1620 carved into it. "No one knows for sure."

"That's Plymouth Rock?" asked Grant, cocking his head to the side. "That's not very big. I thought it would be humongous!"

"Historians believe that this is only about one-third of the rock," said Arabella. "They think souvenir hunters chipped a lot of it away years before this monument was built. A replica of the Mayflower is docked over there," she said, pointing. "Directly across the bay is Provincetown on Cape Cod. The Pilgrims stayed there for a few weeks before they ended their journey here."

"I can't imagine traveling across the ocean in the Mayflower," said Christina. "It was about 90 feet long. That's the distance from home plate to first base! And about 25 feet wide, which is as wide as a two-car garage!

And 102 passengers were crammed on it for two months!"

"I bet they were happy to get off that thing," said Grant. "I would be because I like the wide open spaces," he added, swinging his skinny arms in circles.

"Me, too," chimed in Quincy.

Soon, the sightseers passed through the village of Buzzard's Bay. Grant raised his hands in front of his face and yelled, "Look out for the buzzards!" He and Quincy exploded into spasms of laughter.

Next, they crossed the Cape Cod Canal into Cape Cod. Wide beaches and lofty sand dunes stretched along both sides of the highway. Cozy cottages replaced condominiums. Hardworking fishing boats outnumbered luxurious cruise ships.

Soon, Arabella had another historic adventure in mind. "Sandwich is the oldest town on Cape Cod and one of the oldest in the United States," said Arabella, turning into the Sandwich Glass Museum. "The town is famous for the pressed glass made here since the 1800s."

"Can I get a sandwich? You know, Saaaandwich!" asked Grant, licking his lips.

"Later," Mimi said.

A kaleidoscope of colors dazzled the group as they entered the museum. Sun streamed through a towering wall of windows and lit up hundreds of sparkling glass pieces on display.

"Now, that's what I call bling!" said Mimi.

Christina watched a glassblower artfully blow a large goblet. "Is beach sand used to make glass?" she asked the tour guide.

"No, we import sand. Beach sand is too impure," he replied.

That's crazy, thought Christina. Miles of sand in Massachusetts and it can't be used for making glass.

"Let's eat a sandwich in Sandwich!" said Grant as they left the museum.

"I'm not sure I want a sandwich right now," said Mimi. She pulled her sunglasses from her red rhinestone glass case. "But a dish of praline ice cream would make me happy. I know I can count on Papa for that," she said, winking at her husband.

At the sandwich shop, the kids huddled together in a bright orange booth away from the grownups. Christina dropped two quarters in the jukebox on their table and chose a favorite Beatles song.

"Tell me more about the dunes disappearing," she said as the music began.

"All around our cottage, the dunes aren't as high anymore," said Amelia.

"How can you tell?" asked Grant, biting into his grilled cheese sandwich.

"We just can," said Quincy, shrugging his shoulders. "We can see over them in places where we couldn't before."

"That's right," said Amelia. "A few weeks ago, we couldn't see the ocean behind one particular dune, even when we stood on a chair. Now, it's no problem."

Christina licked the rim of her mint chocolate chip ice cream cone. "Why are you so worried about it?" she asked.

"Because the sand dunes are important to the beach," replied Amelia. She wiped sticky chocolate syrup from her fingers with a napkin. "Dunes help protect the Cape from erosion. The Cape protects the coastline of Massachusetts from storm waves. Someday, thousands of years from now, some scientists think the Cape will completely erode and be **submerged** by the sea."

"That's not good," said Grant, his blue eyes wide with alarm.

"The point is," said Amelia, "the coast erodes at a rate of about three feet a year. We shouldn't be seeing erosion on the dunes like we're seeing now. Arabella's husband, Ben, says we have to protect the dunes. That's why we want you to help us figure out why the dune sand is disappearing."

Christina thoughtfully sipped her water. There was so much sand in her life today. Bags of sand, sand for glass, disappearing sand. What could it possibly mean?

4
THE DOONDWELLERS

Arabella stopped the car at Nauset Light Beach in Cape Cod National Seashore.

"We're almost home," she said, "but I want you to see the beach under a full moon. The storm will be rolling in soon. It will be too cloudy tomorrow."

"Ahhhhhh..." Christina sighed, drinking in the smell of the ocean as the kids hopped out of the car. She gazed up at the dunes **illuminated** by the soft, silvery moonlight. She had not imagined anything like this.

"What do you mean the dunes are disappearing?" whispered Grant to the kids. "They look about 10,000 feet tall to me!"

"As author Henry David Thoreau said, 'A man may stand there and put all America behind him,'" recited Mimi. She slipped off her red sneakers and strolled towards the water.

The kids followed her lead. Soon, they were all wiggling their toes in the moist, chilly sand.

"Did I ever tell you about the dune dwellers in Truro?" Mimi asked.

"What are doondwellers?" asked Grant. "It's two words, Grant," she said. "Dune dwellers are people who live in shacks built on dunes in very remote areas of Cape Cod. Most have lived there for decades. Writers like Tennessee Williams and Eugene O'Neill and a lot of artists stayed in dune dweller shacks for a time."

"What are the shacks like?" asked Christina.

"Some are very primitive," Mimi replied. "Shipwrecked sailors built some of them.   People made others with glass, shingles, and weathered planks of wood. But they have no electricity or running water."

Suddenly, Christina guessed something. "Mimi, did you ever live in a dune shack?" she asked.

"Yes, when I was in Truro," admitted Mimi. "And I really want to see if it's still there!"

Everyone, except Papa, looked awestruck. Papa just leaned back on the heels of his boots, amused by the reaction to Mimi's confession.

"Cool!" Grant cried. "You lived in a dune shack. You were a dune dweller! How did you take a bath?"

Mimi laughed. "I managed," she said.

Christina couldn't imagine anyone living in a shack in the dunes, especially her sassy, red-shoed grandma. It sounded too weird, too creepy, and too mysterious.

Suddenly, Amelia shouted. Christina spun around and glanced at the ocean just in time to see the outline of an enormous whale gliding along the horizon!

"It's a whale! It's a whale!" shouted Grant, dancing and wildly waving his arms up in the air. "We saw a whale!"

Fiery skies, dune dwellers, whale sightings, and disappearing sand. Christina shivered. She felt like this odd concoction of events was leading to something very strange!

5

DISAPPEARING DUNES

Christina awoke to the smell of bacon frying and coffee brewing. Breakfast! She threw on a sweater and jeans. Grabbing her fleece jacket, she bounded across the breezeway that separated her room from Arabella and Ben's cottage.

Even Grant was already at the kitchen table in the sun-filled room. "Oh, no, it's Christina! I thought I was going to get all the bacon," he teased, popping a crispy strip into his mouth.

"Good morning, dear," said Mimi. "Are you hungry? Arabella is treating us to a breakfast fit for a king and his court."

"Good morning, everyone," said Christina, pulling out a cane ladder-back chair. "Thank you, Arabella. I'm starved."

Arabella placed a plate stacked with syrup-drenched French toast on the blue-checked tablecloth in front of Christina. "Dig in," she said, smiling. "There's more syrup and lots of fresh cranberry sauce."

"We've got a fun day ahead of us," said Papa. He folded his newspaper and turned his attention to his French toast.

Christina was cutting her second piece of cranberry-pecan streusel when Amelia and Quincy appeared at the back door.

"Come in, come in," said Arabella. "Would you like some breakfast?"

"No thanks. We ate," said Amelia, "but we do want to introduce our mother to everyone." Mrs. Winthrop was on her way to Nauset Lighthouse to give a tour to a group of visitors.

"That must be a fascinating job," said Papa, who enjoyed poking around old lighthouses.

"I always loved the romance of the lighthouse keeper's job and giving tours is as close as I can get to it," Mrs. Winthrop said. "After Dan died at sea, working at the lighthouse became even more important to me. Amelia," she added, "why don't you bring everyone to the lighthouse this afternoon? The view from the top is just breathtaking!"

"That's my kind of tour," said Papa, "up close and personal!"

"If you kids want to do a little shellfishing this morning, we can have a clambake this evening before the weather gets too windy," Mrs. Winthrop said as she waved goodbye.

"Shellfishing?" asked Grant, looking puzzled. "Can you eat fish shells? Wouldn't they cut your mouth?"

"I'll show you, Grant," said Quincy.

The kids thanked Arabella for the delicious breakfast and raced out the door.

A few yards away from the cottage, Amelia put her hand up. "Stop!" she said. "First, Quincy and I want to show you the dunes that are disappearing."

She turned toward the beach with the kids following on her heels. When they got to the dunes, Amelia said, "Look! This whole row of dunes is much shorter than it was. In fact, this one's even shorter than when Quincy and I inspected it a few days ago."

"It's like someone is scooping sand right off the top of it," said Quincy.

Christina wandered around the huge dunes. She was careful not to disturb any of the vegetation. Since she had not seen the dunes before, it was hard to tell that anything was different.

"Come here!" she called to the others, who came running around the dune. "It's some kind of track!"

The track was about two feet wide and started at the base of the dune.

"It looks like something was dragged from here to over there," said Christina. She pointed in the direction of the track.

Grant, who had followed the track, yelled back. "More tracks! But these are definitely tire tracks!"

6
CLAM HOES AND BUCKETS

It was low tide as the kids waded into the mud flats, wearing sandals and carrying buckets and clam hoes.

"This is the best time for clamming," said Quincy. "Clams live in saltwater, freshwater, and muddy places near the water. They burrow into the sand or mud, and that's where you'll find them."

"I thought we were shellfishing," said Grant, inspecting the prongs on his rake.

"Clams have shells," said Quincy. "Here's a good spot."

Quincy burrowed into the mud with his clam hoe and lifted several, grayish, oval-shaped clams out of the water.

"See how a clam has two oval halves connected by this little joint?" asked Quincy.

"Let me see," said Grant, moving closer to get a good look.

"Once Mother steams them, they'll pop right open," said Quincy. "Then, you just pick out the little clam and eat it!" He pulled a thin, metal ring from his pocket. "If a clam is smaller than this ring," he said, "throw it back in. It's illegal to take it."

Quincy threw one clam back in the water and rinsed off most of the mud on the others. Then he put the clams in his bucket. "We'll let Mother take care of washing them better," he said, mischievously.

"That's it?" asked Grant.

"That's it!" said Amelia. "Just dig them out of their hiding places!"

After several minutes of serious digging, Christina asked, "Why would someone be driving on the dunes?"

"And what were they dragging?" asked Grant, shoving his clam hoe into the mud.

"I can't think of a reason for either," said Amelia. "You used to be able to drive on the beach, but not anymore. There are laws against it in many areas."

Just then, the kids heard a man's voice calling, "Hello, Quincy and Amelia!"

"It's Ben!" said Quincy. He waved his hands wildly. "We haven't seen him for a couple of days."

"You two must be Christina and Grant," Ben said. "I heard you had gone clamming."

"Yes, Mother is having a clambake for us this evening," said Amelia, picking clams out of her hoe full of mud and plopping them in her bucket.

"I do love your mother's clambakes," said Ben. He smiled and put his arm around Amelia. "Are you going to include any lobsters in your clambake?"

"Mother said she would get some," said Amelia.

"How do you catch a lobster?" asked Grant.

"Our father used to set lobster traps," said Amelia. "They're also called lobster pots. Sometimes he would just scuba dive right down and grab one with his hand."

"Wow! I'd like to try that some time," said Grant, impressed.

"You have to be real careful of those big lobster claws!" said Ben. "What else have you all been up to?"

"Just showing our new friends all the things we like to do," said Quincy. A wide grin spread across his freckled face.

"Ben, we have a problem," said Amelia. "We think someone has been messing with the dunes near our house. It looks like the sand is disappearing. This morning, we found a strange track that led to tire tracks."

"Did you tell your mom about it?" Ben asked.

"No, but Christina and Grant know because they were with us this morning," said Amelia.

"They are good at solving mysteries," Quincy added.

"Well, I know that I always tell you to protect the dunes," said Ben, looking serious. "And it's excellent that you are watching them so closely. But it's probably some teenagers goofing around in a dune buggy. Sooner or later, someone will catch them. I wouldn't worry about it too much. I'll check it out the next time I'm around there."

Ben waved goodbye. "See you all later! And have fun!"

"He's got a good point," said Amelia. Her bucket was nearly full of clams.

Christina wiggled her hoe in the mud and pulled out several clams. "Yes, he does," she replied. "Maybe it is a teen in a dune buggy."

But Christina had a feeling there was something more to it!

7

DANCE LIKE A FIDDLER CRAB

Christina, Grant, Amelia, and Quincy were waiting at the trailhead of the Nauset Marsh Trail when Mimi and Papa approached. Mimi pointed to her new, red all-weather hiking sandals. "How do you like them?" she asked, spinning around like a model.

Everyone clapped. "They're cool, Mimi," said Grant. "I wish I had some!"

"How was the clamming?" Papa asked, looking up from the trail guidebook in his hand.

"We got four full buckets," said Quincy. "Mother said it should be plenty for our clambake tonight."

"And we got all the mud off the clams—and ourselves," said Christina. "I hope." She checked her elbows and fingernails as they started to walk.

The day was cool as they hiked through the woods and beside vast, windswept marshes. Christina glimpsed a fox darting through the marsh grass. Amelia spotted a family of rabbits while Mimi stopped to smell the bayberry shrub. Shorebirds coasted lazily over Salt Pond. Quincy identified three different songbirds with his binoculars.

Grant said, "I don't understand what's so important about the marshes. They look pretty dreary to me."

"WHAT?!" everyone else said in unison.

"The marsh is some of the most important land on Earth," said Christina. "It provides food, water, shelter, and habitat for all kinds of wildlife."

"Much of our food chain either begins life in the marsh or depends on what is grown there," Papa explained, "like turtles, fish, shellfish, microscopic plankton, and birds."

"That's because the marsh is rich in nutrients, especially from decaying cord grasses that grow in it," said Amelia.

"It's teeming with life," said Mimi, putting her arm around Grant. "You just have to stop and take a look at it."

Grant, who was hanging his head, spied a fiddler crab waving its one large claw. Grant kicked off his sandals. "Watch this!" he cried. "I'm a Cape Cod crab!" He began imitating the crab. He waved one arm over his head and lumbered around the trail. Not to be left out, Quincy joined in.

"And there's another thing about marshes," said Amelia, as the group giggled at the boys' antics. "They buffer the dunes in a storm. And the dunes help protect our mainland."

As if on cue, the wind swirled around them. PLOP! Christina felt a raindrop just as Grant yelled, "Ouch!"

Grant scooped up the sharp object he had stepped on. Continuing to dance like a fiddler crab, he moved toward Christina and secretly slipped it into her hand.

Christina looked at the empty crab shell Grant had handed her. Written on the **crustacean's** shell was a warning:

Stay away
from the
dunes!

8

THE CRABBY CLUE

Christina flopped onto a bench in front of the Salt Pond Visitor Center at Cape Cod National Seashore. "I need something to drink," she said.

"I need a candy bar," said Grant, plopping down beside her.

"Maybe we can find both in here," said Papa, pointing to the visitor center.

"He's the man with the money," said Mimi. She followed Papa through the door.

Christina and Grant frantically motioned at Amelia and Quincy, who were headed for the door too. "Boy, do we have something," said Grant excitedly. "Look at what I stepped on back on the trail."

They huddled around Christina. She opened up her hand, revealing the shell's message.

"Whew, that is weird!" said Quincy, stepping back.

Just then, a female park ranger stepped outside. "Hi, kids," she said. "I'm Ranger Anna Burnside. I'm a marine biologist here at the national park. I just met your grandparents. Would you like to see some of our natural history exhibits? I think they will tickle your fancy!"

"Tickle my fancy?" Grant whispered to Quincy. "I'm not going to let that lady tickle my anything!"

"Oh, Grant," Amelia said, "that just means you'll like what's inside!"

Christina quickly closed her fist. She saw Ranger Burnside intently staring at her. "We'd love to see the exhibits," Christina said, jumping up.

Ranger Burnside was right. The kids quickly became engrossed in a slide show about the Cape's history and geography.

"Did you know that cranberries don't grow in water like everyone thinks?" asked Mimi. She tapped her red fingernail on an exhibit about local industry.

"How do they grow?" asked Grant. He remembered the cranberry bogs he saw from the *Mystery Girl* when they flew over Cape Cod.

"They grow on vines in impermeable beds layered with sand, peat, gravel, and clay," Mimi explained.

"What does in-per-ma-ble mean, Mimi?" asked Grant.

"It's impermeable," said Mimi. "It means that water can't pass through it."

"So, it's like the cranberries are in a plastic bag of water?" asked Grant.

"I guess you could say that!" Mimi said and laughed. "Anyway, these beds are called bogs. They were originally formed by deposits from glaciers."

Christina absent-mindedly gazed out the large picture window. Gray clouds rolled over the marshes and the Atlantic Ocean. Amelia quietly walked over to Christina and whispered, "I don't know what to think of that note on the shell. Grant's not pulling a joke on us, is he?"

"No," Christina replied. "I don't know where it came from or what it means, but it's definitely not a joke. Grant has his limits," she added, smiling.

She glanced over her shoulder. Ranger Burnside's piercing blue eyes were watching her and Amelia's every move.

9
MYSTERIOUS DISAPPEARANCE

"Now, don't you kids get too far ahead of us," Mimi said good-naturedly. She adjusted the strap on her helmet as Papa held the red bike he had rented for her.

"Oh, they won't go too far ahead," Papa said. "I've got their lunches in my backpack!"

"We'll probably stick to the loop trail," said Christina, studying the trail map. "Plus, I've got my trusty GPS clipped right here to my handlebars!" said Grant. No chance that I'll get lost."

"Guess we'll just follow you," said Christina, folding up the trail map. "Lead the way, little brother! I'll text you when we get to the beach, Mimi!"

The four waved to Mimi and Papa and took off down the Provincetown Trail at Cape Cod National Seashore.

After climbing the third steep hill, they stopped for a rest and to look at the view.

"This trail is a lot of work," said Christina, "but I like it."

"This isn't even the steepest hill," said Quincy, who often rode the trail with his friends and knew the sharp curves and low tunnels of Provincetown Trail by heart. "That's Herring Cove Beach," he said, pointing down toward the ocean.

"Is that like a red herring?" asked Grant. The two boys looked at each other and started giggling. Then Quincy suddenly stopped and said, "What's a red herring?"

"A red herring," said Christina, "is a clue that's supposed to mislead you. Mystery writers use red herrings to make you think someone is a villain when they really aren't."

"Ohhhh!" said Quincy. "I get it."

"Come on, guys. Let's go past the Old Harbor Life-Saving Station," said Amelia. "It's pretty cool. Plus, I want to check on my plant study."

"What's that?" asked Christina.

"It's a project for school," said Amelia. "I picked a dune near the old life-saving station at Race Point Beach. I'm taking photos of the plants growing on it, identifying them, writing up some information, and making a notebook. I'm also looking for things like erosion."

"There might be some erosion after this storm," said Quincy, taking a drink of water from his canteen and glancing up at the sky.

"Yeah, I'm glad we came out here," Amelia said. "It's a good idea to check on it today before the storm comes in. I wish I had my camera."

"Never fear," said Grant, "I've got one on my phone. I'll take a picture for you and email it to you."

"Perfect," said Amelia. "Let's go!"

The kids parked their bikes at the old life-saving station. "This is one of the few stations still standing where nothing has changed since it was built in 1897," Amelia said, scuffing her way to the dunes.

"Oh, no!" she cried and froze in her tracks. Her eyes grew wide and her mouth flew open.

"What's wrong?" asked Christina. "What's wrong?"

"My dune plants are gone," said Amelia, tears welling in her eyes. "I have pictures. I know this is the right dune. About half of it has disappeared!"

Quincy slid beside Amelia and took her hand. "I'm sorry, sis. I know this is the right dune too. What could have happened?"

Grant started snapping pictures of the remaining dune.

"Hey, kids, what are you doing out here?" a familiar voice said. It was Ben.

"Amelia's dune is gone," said Grant. "We're trying to find it."

Amelia told Ben her story and he tried to console her. "Look how strong the wind blows out here," he said. "These dunes are just eroding. A big wind has probably been beating away at it every hour since you were last here. All that sand is just blowing away to another part of the Cape."

"You think so?" said Amelia.

"I'm sorry," said Ben, giving Amelia a little hug. "I'm doing some maintenance work at the life-saving station. I've got to get back over there. Just pick another dune for your study. You all be careful; the weather is going to get a lot rougher before long."

Christina stared at Amelia's damaged dune. Ben said the sands are blowing away and relocating. But are they?

10
SAND, SAND, SAND!

Christina carefully lifted the plastic lid off her cup of steaming chowder. She counted six tender clams floating on the top. "This smells great," she said. She breathed in the hearty aroma. "Mimi always knows exactly what we need."

"She's the best grandma!" Grant said. He settled the ear buds of his iPod in place and opened his box lunch. "Everyone needs a Mimi!"

"By the way, where did she go?" asked Amelia.

"She and Papa are eating their lunches on the deck of the Province Lands Visitor Center," Christina replied. "Mimi said it has a great view, and she doesn't care for sand in her chowder." Christina quickly covered her own soup as a gust of wind swirled sprinkles of sand around her.

The next few minutes were spent in silence. The four kids sat on the beach and devoured the clam-chocked chowder, juicy fried oyster sandwiches, and crispy french fries.

Suddenly, Grant blurted out, "You are the dancing queen, young and sweet, only 17!" Quincy sprang to his feet. He spun and twirled while Grant continued to sing.

"He has *Dancing Queen* on his iPod?" asked Amelia. She raised her eyebrows at Christina.

Christina shrugged. "Go figure," she said, licking french fry salt from her fingers.

Christina collected the empty lunch boxes and dumped them into a nearby trash container. "OK, everyone," she said. She gestured to Grant and Quincy to stop dancing.

"Circle the wagons! We need to discuss these clues before Mimi and Papa come after us."

Everyone sat criss-cross in the sand. Christina removed the crab shell clue from her jacket pocket and laid it in the middle of the group.

"Here's what we have," she said, brushing a wisp of hair off her face. "First, Amelia and Quincy believe the dunes near their house are disappearing. Next, we saw a strange track, leading to a tire track in the sand."

"Ben thinks it's a dune buggy track," Quincy said.

"Right. Then, we have this crab shell warning us to stay away from the dunes," said Christina.

"That I stepped on!" said Grant, joyfully.

"That Grant stepped on," said Christina. She patted his head.

"And the plants I was studying for my school project are gone from my dune!" said Amelia, wringing her hands. "I have to start all over again!"

"Now, Ben said that dune sands shift," said Christina, "and I remember hearing that in school. But I also remember that vegetation stabilizes a coastal dune."

"Does that mean plants help hold the dune sand in place?" asked Grant.

"Right," said Christina. "So even if the sand blows away from the dune, the plants shouldn't blow away, too. Something or someone had to mess with your dune and your plants, Amelia."

For several minutes, all four kids sat deep in thought.

"Plus," said Christina, wrinkling her nose, "that park ranger really gives me a creepy feeling."

Suddenly, a gust of wind flung sand in Christina's face. When she opened her eyes, Ranger Anna Burnside towered above the circle of friends. Christina's jaw dropped wide open. She scooped up the shell and put it in her pocket.

"Did you kids have a good bike ride today?" asked Ranger Burnside, curtly.

"Yes, we did," said Christina. She jumped up and briskly brushed the sand from her clothes.

"I guess you saw a lot of interesting things along the bike trail?" asked Ranger Burnside, putting her hands on her hips.

"Yes, ma'am," said Amelia. "We showed them the old life-saving station and the dunes at Race Point Beach."

Ranger Burnside squinted her eyes at them and folded her arms across her chest. "Have you kids been playing on the dunes?" she asked.

"No, ma'am!" the four kids said in unison.

"We respect the dunes," said Amelia. She was offended that anyone would think she was playing on the dunes

"Well, make sure you stay off them," the ranger warned. "I'll be watching. We don't need a bunch of **disobedient** kids hanging out on the dunes." She spun around and walked back down the beach.

Sand stung Christina's face a second time. "Great! Now there's sand in my eyes," she muttered, blinking and tearing up. She zipped up her jacket and hugged her arms.

Something is wrong, she thought. I bet Ranger Burnside has something to do with it.

11
BAM! BAM!

The sound of wind in Christina's ears turned into the sound of hammers as she and the kids traipsed through the sand back to Ben and Arabella's cottage. All over Cape Cod, people were boarding up their homes and businesses. A nor'easter was approaching!

"Eg-sactly what is a nor'easter?" asked Grant. "It's fall. It's not Easter time."

Quincy giggled. "It doesn't have to be Easter," he said. "They can happen about anytime."

"Nor'easters are really terrible storms or hurricanes," said Amelia. "They usually form from hot and cold air over the Atlantic Ocean. Then they blow from the northeast into Cape Cod and the rest of the Massachusetts coastline. That's how nor'easters got their name. Mother always tells us to prepare for the worst and hope for the best!"

BAM! BAM! Ben drove in the last nail in a wooden storm shutter on the front porch. The kids heard him say, "Once and for all, we are not selling!" just as they walked up. Mrs. Eleanor Gage, a lady who lived down the road, glared at the children, spun around, and huffed down the walkway. She banged the white, wooden gate behind her.

"When's the nor-easter going to hit?" asked Grant. He was excited about all the storm activity and oblivious to the scene that he had just witnessed.

"Sometime tomorrow," said Arabella, who was moving wicker furniture off the porch. "We're getting ready so we don't have to do it at the last minute. Ben's secured his boats. Now, we're storm-proofing the cottage so we'll all stay safe and dry."

"It's getting colder already," said Amelia.

"Is it going to snow?" asked Christina.

"The Weather Channel forecasted only rain," said Papa, coming out of the cottage. "But there will be a lot of it."

"Have you ever been in a nor'easter or a hurricane?" Amelia asked Christina.

"No, not even close," said Christina. "Sometimes we get the remnants of rain from a hurricane or tropical storm. But in Peachtree City, Georgia, we're pretty far away from both the Atlantic Coast and the Gulf Coast."

Mimi stepped onto the porch, her red backpack slung over her shoulder. "Did Papa tell you that we've decided to go to Truro now and come back tomorrow before the storm hits?" asked Mimi, looking at Christina and Grant. "Go pack your pajamas and some warm clothes for tomorrow."

Startled, Christina, Grant, Amelia, and Quincy looked at each other. If Christina and

Grant had to go to Truro, they might not get the mystery solved!

"Mimi," said Christina, using her best pleading voice, "we would love to see where you used to live, but can we stay with Amelia and Grant? We are having such a good time. And Mrs. Winthrop wants to take us to the top of the lighthouse. And we want to eat the clams we caught. Remember, Mrs. Winthrop is planning a clambake tonight. And ..."

Mimi threw her hand out like a traffic guard stopping traffic. "Whoa," she said and started to laugh. "No need to go on. You can stay if it's all right with Ben and Arabella."

"Could they please have a sleepover with us?" Amelia asked. "I can text Mother and ask right now."

"Mimi, they're welcome to spend the night here or with the children if Mrs. Winthrop okays it," said Arabella. "Ben and I would love it."

"Mother says fine," sang out Amelia, holding up her phone for everyone to see for proof: yes and we will have r clambake 2night:).

"Well, Papa, it looks like we'll be exploring on our own," said Mimi, handing her backpack to Papa.

"Sounds good to me," said Papa. "Let's get going. You kids behave yourself, and we'll see you tomorrow. Unless we decide to become dune dwellers!"

Later, Christina was stuffing pajamas into her overnight bag when she heard voices, low but growing louder as they came closer. It was Ben and Arabella. Now they had stopped in the breezeway right outside her boarded-up window.

"Ben, how are we going to pay our bills?" Christina heard Arabella ask. "It would relieve a lot of pressure if we sold to Mrs. Gage. You're so stressed out all the time. You're not yourself! I don't want to leave the Cape either, but maybe we need to try something different. And Mrs. Gage is right, this cottage would make a beautiful bed and breakfast."

"We are not leaving the Cape, Arabella," said Ben firmly.

BAM! BAM! Ben hit another nail in the storm shutter of Christina's room. She jumped liked she'd been hit with a board.

"I'm not going to say it again," Ben said angrily. "We love it here. We would be miserable if we left and you know it. I'll figure it out!"

Christina heard Ben's heavier footsteps walk down the breezeway and a fainter "BAM! BAM!" several feet away. She zipped up her bag. Her tummy did a flip-flop. She hated to overhear her new friends arguing. She couldn't imagine having to move from her own home. She felt terrible for Ben and Arabella and wished she could help them. Christina wished she could help Amelia and Quincy solve their mystery too. But right now, nothing made sense. Her tummy flip-flopped again.

12

SANDCASTLE
WARNINGS

Amelia and Christina dragged Amelia's little **skiff** to the Winthrop's back deck. Amelia took the thick rope hanging from the bow of the boat and tied it securely to a post.

"What kind of knot is that?" asked Christina, impressed with Amelia's skill.

"It's called a bowline," said Amelia. "Sailors use it a lot to rig sailboats. My father always said if you were marooned on a desert island and could only take one knot with you, this would be the one!"

"Was this his boat?" asked Christina.

"Actually, he built it for me for my sixth birthday," Amelia replied. "We used to row it around the inlets and marshes all the time." She tucked two oars inside the skiff and patted the knot. "There, it'll stay tight in the storm."

Just then, Grant and Quincy skipped down the steps of the cottage. Grant had tied the short side of a beach towel around his neck, like a cape. The wind snapped the lime-green towel wildly as Grant pretended to fly like Superman. He stopped short in front of the girls and stuck a codfish-shaped mask in front of his face. "I'm a cape cod!" he cried.

"That's great, Grant," said Christina, trying not to laugh.

"Look!" Grant said. "It's the menu I colored at the restaurant. I just taped a Popsicle stick to it like a handle. See? Pretty good, huh?"

"Don't laugh, Amelia. It only encourages him!" said Christina.

Grant held the mask up to his face again and the girls started giggling in spite of themselves.

"Let's go build a sandcastle," said Christina. She was still worried about Ben and Arabella's argument and wanted to do something fun.

"We've got some great sandcastle molds," said Amelia. She reached under the deck and pulled out a mesh bag. "Let's go!"

The four scampered to the beach and began digging into the wet, cold sand. Amelia dumped out the bag of molds while Grant and Quincy pushed sand into a huge mound. Christina firmly packed sticky sand into her coffee-can mold. Before long, a four-towered sandcastle was taking shape.

"Let's dig a moat around it!" Quincy yelled, plunging his shovel into the sand.

"It's almost time to go to the lighthouse," said Amelia. "Mother wants to take us up to the top before it gets dark."

"I'll get some water to wash off our hands," said Christina, grabbing a sunshine-yellow plastic bucket and running down to the ocean. She spit a little sand from her teeth and laughed. Sand again, she thought.

Suddenly, Christina stopped in her tracks and gasped. Turning toward the other kids, she yelled, "Come here! Quick!"

Written in the sand in deep, thick, block letters was a warning.

Goosebumps broke out on Christina's arms and she shivered. Who was following them?

13
FALLING INTO THE SEA

Christina gazed up at Nauset Lighthouse towering 48 feet above the cliffs of Nauset Light Beach. Its bottom half was painted stark white and the top half was cherry red. This part of Cape Cod had always been one of the most dangerous for sailors, and the wreckage of countless boats covered the ocean floor. But the lighthouse had also steered many sailors and fishermen to safety.

"Now I remember why this lighthouse looks so familiar," said Christina as the kids approached the base of the building. "It's the lighthouse on bags of Cape Cod Potato Chips!"

"Yes, it is!" said Quincy. "It's famous!"

"Welcome to the lighthouse!" said Mrs. Winthrop as she opened the door and greeted the kids.

"Awesome!" said Grant. "That's a tall staircase! How many stairs are there?"

"Forty-four," said Mrs. Winthrop. "Believe me, I know!"

Mrs. Winthrop picked up her old metal lantern and said, "Are you ready to go to the top?"

"Whoopee!" shouted Grant. "After you, Mrs. Lightkeeper!" he added, with a deep bow.

Mrs. Winthrop led the way up the brick-red spiral staircase. "This lighthouse is more than 100 years old," she said. "The outside shell is made of cast iron. The inside is brick and it has a slate roof." She pointed straight up. "The light alternates red and white flashes every five seconds. Even on a foggy night, sailors can see it a mile or so out from the shore."

Christina gasped when she got to the top. She could see bobbing whitecaps on the Atlantic Ocean, grassy marshes, weathered Cape Cod cottages snuggled into inlets and hills, and fishing boats returning from a hard day's work. Above it all, the rolling, gray clouds reminded everyone that a storm was approaching.

"See those steps going down to the beach?" asked Amelia, pointing to the wooded plank walkway. "Every time we have a bad storm, they get totally smashed up! Hopefully, they won't look like toothpicks this time tomorrow!"

"The stairs aren't the only thing a nor'easter destroys," said Mrs. Winthrop. "See that red and white post on the edge of the cliff? That's where this lighthouse used to stand. They moved it here about 10 years ago."

"Why was it so close to the cliff?" asked Grant. "Wouldn't it fall into the ocean?"

"It would have," said Mrs. Winthrop. "That's why it was moved to where it stands now. When the lighthouse was first built in that place where the post is, it was 200 feet away from the edge of the cliff. Strong storm waves pound against the bottom of the cliff, gouge out big chunks of sand, and carry the sand out to sea. The sand above the gouge becomes unstable and falls down the cliff to the beach. Soon, the rest of the bank above the gouge, including grass, shrubs, and trees, breaks off and falls onto the beach too."

"Wow!" said Grant. "I'd like to see that happen."

"Eventually, the sand smoothes itself out and looks just like it did before," said Amelia. "The only difference is that the edge of the cliff is now several feet closer to the lighthouse."

"So the waves keep eating away at the sandy shore and the cliff keeps eroding out from under the lighthouse," said Christina. "And that's how the waves erode the rest of the shoreline, too."

"That's correct," said Mrs. Winthrop. "It's not a happy thought. Cape Cod is a narrow strip of land. One of these days, it won't be here. There's an exhibit about it in the old brick oil house."

"What is that house over there?" asked Christina, pointing to a red-roofed house next to the lighthouse.

"That's the keeper's house," Mrs. Winthrop replied. "It's been moved a couple of times as well."

"Yikes!!" said Grant. "What if you were sleeping one night and your bed fell off the cliff?"

"That's not a happy thought either," said Mrs. Winthrop, smiling and shaking her brown curls.

"Why don't you or someone else live in the keeper's house?" asked Christina.

"In the old days, being a lighthouse keeper was a full time job and very necessary," said Mrs. Winthrop. "You had to be here all day and all night to make sure the oil light didn't go out. That's why the keeper lived next to the lighthouse."

"Keepers lived here with their families," added Amelia. "And sometimes they didn't see anybody else for weeks."

"I still look after everything," said Mrs. Winthrop. "And I give tours of the lighthouse, the oil house museum, and the keeper's house. But it's no longer necessary for anyone to live here."

"Wow, if your mom was the keeper, you would've lived here in the old days," said Grant to Quincy. "How cool is that?"

"It would be scary," said Quincy, nervously.

"In fact, with all our modern electronic navigational devices, lighthouses aren't as important as they once were," said Mrs. Winthrop. "But this light is a private aid to navigation now and guides fishing boats, kayakers, and others who navigate close to the shore."

"Like our father," said Amelia. "We would row my little skiff around here. He always called this Mother's Lighthouse. He said we could always count on this lighthouse to keep us from getting lost."

"Now I love lighthouses as much as Papa does," said Christina. She put her arm around Amelia's shoulders.

After they carefully walked back down the spiral steps, Mrs. Winthrop showed the kids an enormous light bulb. "This is just like the one that lights up the top of the lighthouse," she said.

"Just think," said Grant, "if we had one of these, we'd only need one light bulb for our whole house!"

"Here's a flashlight for each of you in case you need it later," said Mrs. Winthrop, placing her lantern in its customary spot near the stairway. "Let's go! The clambake should be ready by now!"

Christina thought the surf sounded louder and rougher. She could see the clambake fire pit glowing as they ambled down the wooden steps that led to the beach below. A jumble of thoughts tumbled through her head. Would these steps still be here tomorrow night after this monster of a storm blew in? Would the post that marked the lighthouse's old location tumble into the sea? Did Amelia's dune really disappear or was it just nature and the passing of time? And who wanted them to stay away?

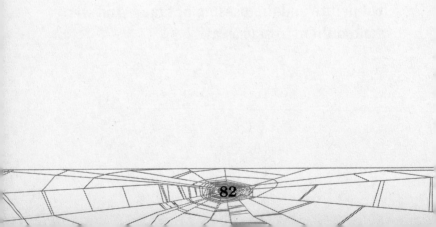

14

SEAWEED AND SEAWATER

Earlier that day, Mrs. Winthrop had dug a pit into the sand just below the cliffs. She filled it with a tight layer of rocks and built a fire. When the rocks were scorching hot, she removed the burning wood and ashes and placed a thick layer of fresh, moist seaweed on top of the steaming, hot rocks. Then, she added the clams the kids had dug, plus mussels, a couple of lobsters, corn, potatoes, and onions. She poured sea water on it and let it cook the rest of the afternoon.

The kids stood over the fire pit, checking out the concoction of shellfish and vegetables. "Are we going to eat seaweed?" Grant asked, horrified.

"No, no! The seaweed helps to cook the food," said Mrs. Winthrop, pouring sea water on the clambake.

Grant jumped back with his mouth wide open, unable to say a word.

"Don't worry, Grant, you can't taste the sea water," said Quincy. "Trust me."

Soon, the kids were sitting around the fire pit and eating their clambake from big metal bowls. "I never knew something that was dug out of the mud and cooked in seaweed and sea water could taste so good," said Christina. She dunked a juicy clam into a fragrant mixture of melted butter and lemon juice.

Grant nodded and creamy blobs of potato escaped from between his lips.

"What were those three lighthouses in a row that we passed coming here?" Christina asked, pointing toward Nauset Light.

"Those are the very first lighthouses built along this beach," said Amelia, digging a mussel out of its shell. "They're called the Three Sisters. They're about 200 years old. They don't work anymore. They were moved from the edge of the cliff and placed back there a long time ago."

Mrs. Winthrop got up and shuffled through the sand back to the lighthouse. "I've got a special treat for dessert," she called over her shoulder. "I'll be right back."

"I hope it's brownies with chocolate icing and nuts!" said Quincy, rubbing his hands together and smacking his lips.

Christina watched as Mrs. Winthrop climbed the stairs. "I still can't put two and two together on this mystery," she said. "We see how erosion is happening all around us. So, in a way, I think that's what's happening to your dunes, Amelia."

"But why do we keep getting messages telling us to stay off the dunes?" asked Grant. "We haven't played on the dunes. Why is someone trying to scare us away from them?"

"I don't knooooow," moaned Christina, putting her head in her hands.

But Grant was right, she thought. They hadn't climbed any dunes at all. Why would someone try to scare them away? There's got to be more to it than meets the eye.

15
THREE SISTERS AND A SHOVEL

Quincy and Grant raced back and forth between the pit and the ocean, lugging buckets of water to douse the fire.

"That should be good," said Mrs. Winthrop, covering the rocks in the pit with sand. She wiped her hands on her jeans and picked up the lighthouse lantern. "Amelia, did you and Christina take all the metal bowls and utensils to my car?"

"Yes, ma'am," said Amelia. "Is there anything else you want us to do?"

"No, that's good," said Mrs. Winthrop. "It's really starting to get chilly, isn't it? Do you all want to ride back home in the car with me?"

"We'll walk," said Amelia, pulling a blue knit cap out of her jacket pocket and shoving it down over her curly head. "Christina wants to see the Three Sisters up close."

"That's fine," said Mrs. Winthrop. "I'm going to put the lantern away, lock up the lighthouse, and drive home. I expect you to meet me there by 7:00. I'm responsible for you all, and it's time to get inside for the night. Do you have your cell phone, Amelia?"

"Right here," said Amelia, patting her jacket pocket.

"Do you have the flashlights I gave you?" asked Mrs. Winthrop. "It will be getting dark by the time you get home."

"Got 'em!" said the four in unison, scrambling off in the direction of the three lighthouses.

Much shorter than the Nauset Light, the Three Sisters Lighthouses stood in a row at the edge of a wooded area behind the dune ridge.

"These are weird," said Grant, walking up to the middle sister. "They look like they're wearing white dresses and black hats."

"That's how some people think they got the name Three Sisters," said Amelia. "But others say it was mainly because the keeper at that time had three daughters."

"I wonder what it was like to live out here in this wilderness 200 years ago," said Christina. "I sure wouldn't want to be out here in the dark." She backed up a few paces to get a better look at the three lighthouses in a row. Just then, she stumbled on something and tumbled to the ground. " Ouch!" she cried.

"Are you okay?" yelled Grant. The three kids ran to help her.

"Yeah, but what is this?" she said, rubbing her elbow and looking down at the object she had tripped over.

"It's a shovel with a red handle," said Quincy, picking it up.

Christina stood up, brushing sticky sand from her jeans. "Look over here," she said, limping toward the dune ridge. "Someone's been digging in the dunes."

Christina's phone beeped, and everyone jumped. "It's a text from Mimi," she said. "Bet the clambake was great. Will be back in the morning. Get some sleep!"

"Sorry, Mimi," Christina said to the group as she typed in "OK" and hit SEND. "Sleep can wait. We have to figure this out!"

"But not right this minute. We better get home," said Amelia. "Mother means business when she says get home on time!"

The kids looked at each other, knowing what they had to do later tonight.

16
SCRAAAAPE, PLUNK!!

The clouds were thick. There wasn't even a glimmer of moonlight as the kids made their way back to the Three Sisters Lighthouses after Mrs. Winthrop went to bed. Amelia, who knew the path to the lighthouses by heart, led the way. The others followed behind, holding hands and trying not to trip over each other.

"We can turn on our flashlights now," said Amelia. "We're out of sight of the house. It sure is dark!"

Four flashlights clicked on, eerily lighting up four nervous faces in the night.

"Our mom would kill us if she knew we were doing this," said Quincy.

Grant nodded. "Mimi too," he said.

"OK, Amelia," said Christina. "We will follow you. Let's not stop until we get to the lighthouses. Keep close together. No lagging behind."

"Don't worry," said Grant under his breath. "You couldn't shake me with a stick." No one laughed.

When the kids got to the edge of the woods behind the Three Sisters, Amelia abruptly stopped. "Do you hear that?" she whispered.

Except for the crashing of waves on the shore in the distance, the night was still. Suddenly, they heard a scraping noise and a plunk. Then again, a scrape and a plunk.

"Kill the lights," ordered Christina. Four clicks. Darkness.

Scraaaaaape, plunk!

"What's that?" asked Grant.

"It sounds like someone shoveling something," whispered Christina. "Stay here!" She crouched down and edged out around the middle sister lighthouse.

Scraaaaaape, plunk!

The Nauset Lighthouse beacon flashed an alternating red and white light that cast a warm glow in the foggy sky. Christina's eyes grew more accustomed to the darkness. She glimpsed a shadowy movement near the top of the dunes. It had to be a person, but it was impossible to tell anything else.

She eased back to the kids. "Someone is definitely digging on the dunes, but I can't see a thing. We need to get closer," she whispered.

"I'm not so sure that's a good idea," said Quincy, his voice quivering.

"No, it probably isn't a good idea for all of us to go," agreed Christina. "Amelia, you hide in the woods with Quincy. Grant and I have done this type of thing before. We'll try to get closer," she said.

"No, I have to go with you," said Amelia, grabbing Christina's arm. "I'm the only one who can lead you through the darkness."

"You have a good point," said Christina. "Grant, you'll need to stay with Quincy."

"Wait a minute, Christina. I want to go too. I can do it," said Quincy, sliding the hood of his jacket up over his head.

"OK, let's get going," said Christina. "Stay low and stay together!"

Amelia led them around the base of the third sister. Crouching low, they dashed across the open area in front of the Three Sisters. They dove to the dune line, just to the right of the mysterious figure.

Scraaaaape, plunk!! Scraaaaape, plunk!

The noise was so close it made the hair stand up on the back of Christina's neck. Except for a small, glowing light sitting on the dune and the continual red and white flash of the Nauset Lighthouse beacon, the kids couldn't see anything.

Amelia whispered in Christina's ear, "Maybe we can see something from the top of the lighthouse."

Christina nodded and Amelia led the kids across the row of dunes to the lighthouse door.

"I can't find Mother's keys," she whispered. "She always keeps them on a hook under this ledge."

"I don't hear the scraping noise anymore!" whispered Grant.

"Hurry, Amelia! That little red glow is moving over the dunes!" said Christina. "It looks like it's coming this way!"

Amelia frantically fumbled under the ledge for the missing key. "Hurry, Amelia!" said Quincy. He leaned against the door and tumbled inside.

"Someone has already unlocked it!" said Amelia. She scooped up Quincy and the kids scurried inside the lighthouse. "Hurry, hurry!" Christina urged. She closed the door behind them and Amelia led them to a dark cubbyhole at the base of the spiral staircase.

CREEEAAAAKKK! The door to the lighthouse slowly creaked open. The kids huddled together. "Don't breathe," whispered Christina, clutching Grant's hand. Heavy footsteps entered the lighthouse and stomped toward them. The red glow swung to and fro.

Closer. Closer. There was a clank of metal and then another. Suddenly, the glow was gone. The footsteps walked back across the room. CLICK. The door closed, and a key turned in the lock.

17
WATCH OUT
FOR THE SIGN!

For what seemed like hours, the four kids crowded together at the base of the spiral staircase in the Nauset Lighthouse. The wind rattled the door and the surf pounded the shore. The low boom of a foghorn occasionally broke the monotony. All the while, the rotating red and white beacon filled the upper reaches of the lighthouse with a fiery, white glow.

Finally, Christina said, "I don't think I'm scared anymore." She moved out from behind the staircase. Still clutching her hand, Grant followed. Then Amelia shuffled out, her arm around Quincy.

Without a sound, the kids crossed the room. Christina carefully opened the door and peeked out. No one. She stepped outside and a frigid breeze stung her face. Amelia reached under the ledge and retrieved the lighthouse key, which was now hanging on its customary hook. She locked the door and returned the key to its home.

"I'm ready to go back to your house," said Grant.

"Me, too," said Quincy.

Holding hands, the kids dashed back around the sand dunes, across the open space in front of the Three Sisters, and down the path that led to the Winthrop's home.

"I need to catch my breath," said Christina, slowing down to a walk.

"You know, I'm beginning to see pretty good in this pitch black dark," said Grant, trying to forget how scared he had just been.

Christina turned on her flashlight. "Let's only have one light on," she said. "Just to be safe." Bunched together, they strode quickly toward home. The yellowish beam of Christina's flashlight led the way.

The pounding of Christina's heart was almost back to normal when her flashlight illuminated a cardboard sign sticking straight up in the sand in the middle of the path.

The kids careened down the path at breakneck speed and never slowed down until they opened the door of the Winthrop home.

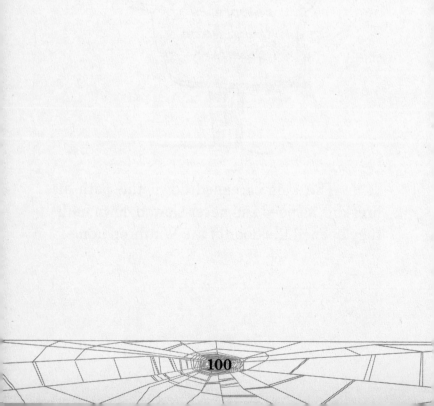

18
SINGING WHALES

Early the next morning, the four kids sat bleary-eyed on the dock of Captain Bob's Whale Watching Cruise in Barnstable. The dock bustled with tourists who were busily buying tickets and waiting to board the *Magical Whale Watcher*. This huge, three-deck, blue and white cruiser would soon take them on the trip of a lifetime.

"I have the feeling someone stayed up too late playing games last night," said Papa cheerily. He stuffed six tickets for the whale watching expedition into the front pocket of his black winter vest and opened the brochure to see what to expect. "Hope you all remembered to put on your long underwear!"

Mimi stared hard at Christina and took a sip from her steaming mug of coffee. "I thought you all would be excited about this trip," she remarked. "I'm sorry it's so early, but the boat goes out with the tides. The captain said this would be the last trip until after the nor'easter rolls through."

"You're right, Papa," said Christina. She cupped her hands around her mug of frothy hot chocolate. "We did stay up too late. And we are very excited, Mimi, just a little sleepy." She had always wanted to go whale watching, but still felt a little stunned by last night's adventure.

"All aboard!" Captain Bob yelled through his bullhorn. "All aboard for an awe-inspiring, breathtaking, and magical experience!"

"OK," said Grant, stretching and yawning. "I'm ready to see some whales."

The four kids leaned against the rail at the bow of the cruiser, away from Mimi and Papa who were busily taking photos. The boat's horn blasted a long goodbye toot as it pulled away. Christina turned around to watch the weathered blue and grey wooden houses of Barnstable shrink in the distance as the ship headed for the open sea.

"Boy, in that lighthouse, we were crammed like Pilgrims in the Mayflower," said Grant. He pulled his brown knit cap down over his ears and rubbed his gloved hands together. "I'm not ready to laugh about it yet," said Christina. "I'm still shaking."

"Who do you think it was?" Amelia asked.

"I don't know," said Christina. "Whoever it was, they knew where your mother keeps her key. And that red glow was her lantern."

"You don't think it's a friend of our mother, do you?" asked Quincy. He was obviously upset that Christina would think his mother was involved.

"Of course not, Quincy," said Christina. "I'm just trying to piece this all together."

"And what about the dune dweller sign?" said Grant. "Maybe it was someone who lives in the dunes."

"Who lives in the dunes?" asked Mimi, walking up to the group.

"Did you meet anyone who lives in the dunes while you were in Truro?" Grant quickly asked his grandma.

"We did! We had a great time," said Mimi. She squeezed in between Grant and Christina and grasped the ship's rail with her red-gloved hands. "We saw the dune shack where I lived. Papa snapped some great photos. But let's talk about whales right now! Didn't you read *Moby-Dick* last year, Christina?"

"I did, and I loved it!" said Christina. "Captain Ahab thinks that *Moby-Dick* represents all that is wrong with the world. He thinks that it's his destiny to kill this symbol of evil. But to me, a whale is what's good with the world. It's a symbol of the power of nature."

"Wow, Christina," said Quincy. "That makes sense to me!"

Mimi smiled. Just then, Papa yelled, "Everyone turn around and let me take a picture!" Papa snapped several shots of the group on the bow of the boat with the ocean spray splashing about them.

"Attention everyone!" the boat speakers screeched. "We are entering whale country. We'll be slowing down our engines. The waves are rougher than normal because of the approaching storm. But we saw lots of whale activity here yesterday. So, keep your eyes open!"

As soon as the cruiser's engines slowed, a long, loud, low-pitched and mysterious wail could be heard in the distance.

"Is that a whale song?" asked Christina, who had heard it on a recording in her science class.

"That's it!" said Mimi, listening and smiling. "Only the male sings, but it can last 10 minutes or more. Scientists don't really know why they sing. But they do know that the whale makes the noise by forcing air through his huge nasal cavities."

Suddenly, the speaker blared again, "Humpback whales starboard!"

"Which way is starboard?" shouted Grant.

"To the right! To the right!" yelled Amelia, pointing that way.

In the distance, several massive humpback whales leaped in and out of the water as if they were playing. The kids screeched in delight as the whales smashed back into the sea, sending cascades of white foam shooting into the air.

"Look at that!" screamed Grant. "It's huuumongous!!"

"How big is a whale?" Quincy asked Papa.

"Adult whales are as much as 50 feet long and they weigh about 80,000 pounds," said Papa. "Even a newborn whale calf is about 15 feet long and weighs about a ton!"

"It's just about time for the whales to swim south for the winter," said Amelia.

"Don't they come to the colder water to eat all summer long and then go to the warmer water in the winter to have their babies?" asked Christina.

"That's right," said Amelia. "And during the winter, they don't eat at all. They just live off their fat!"

"Wow, just like a bear!" said Grant. "Humpbacks port side!" blasted the speaker again.

"Which way?" yelled Grant, looking in all directions.

"To the left, Grant!" Amelia yelled back, pointing as an enormous whale in the distance flipped its gigantic tail, spewing water in all directions.

"I knew that!" said Grant, spinning around.

For the next hour, the cruiser drifted and the kids continued to watch the whales frolicking in the whitecaps. Suddenly, a monster wave smashed the bow of the cruiser, tossing a spray of seawater as high as the second deck. More giant, rolling waves followed. The captain announced that they would have to cut the trip short and head back to Barnstable.

"I sure was hoping we would see a whale a little closer," said Christina as the cruiser slowly began to turn port side. Suddenly, just a few yards from them, the knobby head of a mammoth humpback whale rose out of the water like an alien emerging from another world. Awestruck, the group watched as the whale lifted nearly all of its rippled body out of the water before twisting and splashing down on its back.

Icy cold seawater drenched Grant's face. "This is greaaaaat!!" he yelled. "A whale just gave me a bath!"

Everyone cheered as the cruiser picked up its pace. Christina tightened her wool scarf around her neck and shoved her hands deep into her fleece jacket to get her gloves. Seeing that whale was a good sign, she thought.

That's when she felt a piece of paper. It was the note she had pulled off the bottom of Grant's shoe on the first day of their trip. She read it again.

TONIGHT-
100 bags of sand

Why did she feel that this note had suddenly become more important?

19
MACARONI SHELLS

All over Cape Cod, Christina could hear the pounding of the surf, but the roar was especially loud at Marconi Beach. Waves smashing the shore were several feet high now. They scattered seashells like confetti on the sand beneath the towering dunes.

"I can't believe we haven't gone shelling," said Mimi. She pulled the collar of her red wool jacket up around her ears. "But we picked the perfect day and the perfect place to do it."

"I've never seen so many shells," said Christina. "The storm is really churning them up." She stooped to inspect an unusually large scallop shell.

Grant and Quincy ran ahead, seeing how close they could get to the waves without actually being submerged by the frigid, foaming water.

Grant turned around, his jacket whipping in the wind. "What did you say the name of this beach is?" he yelled, trying to be heard above the roar of the surf. "Macaroni?"

"No! Marconi," Papa yelled back. "Marconi Beach! It's named after the famous Italian inventor Guglielmo Marconi. This is where they transmitted the first transatlantic wireless message between the United States and England in 1903. 'Greetings from President Theodore Roosevelt to the King of England!' Remember? I mentioned it on the plane coming in."

"He did what?" screamed Grant. He cupped his hand to his ear.

"They transmitted..." yelled Papa. "Oh, never mind. We'll talk about it later." He gave Grant a thumbs up.

"What??" yelled Grant again, both hands up to his ears.

Amelia was walking next to Papa. "The transmission station built here," she said, "was also one of the first to receive distress signals from the *Titanic* before it sank."

"Really?" said Papa, examining a bumpy oyster shell. "Now that's very interesting. Mimi loves anything about the *Titanic*. Don't you, my dear?"

Mimi smiled and squeezed her husband's hand.

Christina was hunched down, picking sand dollars out of seaweed when she recognized a person hastily walking toward them. It was Ranger Anna Burnside.

Mimi waved. "Hello, Ranger Burnside," said Mimi. "It's nice to see you again."

"You, too, ma'am. There are a lot of good shells washing up on the beach because of the storm," said Ranger Burnside. She eyed

Christina. "Have you found anything unusual, Christina?"

"Nothing unusual, just some nice starfish," Christina replied. She carefully placed a perfect, white starfish in her shell bag.

"Sometimes we forget that seashells that wash up along our coastal beaches were once part of a living animal that is now dead," said Ranger Burnside. "What we think of as just a seashell was once the outer protective covering of a mollusk." Ranger Burnside continued to direct her remarks to Christina.

Christina stood up. "I learned in science class that a mollusk is a general group of marine invertebrates that includes snails, clams, oysters, and mussels. Is that right, Ranger Burnside?"

"Excellent, Christina! The shell remains long after the animal's death," she said. A slow smile crept across her face. "Well, everyone stay safe and out of the storm. It's going to be a pretty messy one when it gets here."

She turned away and continued striding down the beach.

Amelia cut her eyes toward Christina. "And don't play on the dunes," she mouthed to Christina.

"Did I tell you I ate seaweed at the clambake, Mimi?" yelled Grant. "And I drank seawater!" He sprinted toward them with a wet glob of greenish-yellow seaweed in both hands.

"No, I hadn't heard that yet, dear," said Mimi.

"Only kidding!" said Grant. He tossed the seaweed back into the waves and hugged his grandma around the waist.

Christina gave him a look that said, "We need to talk." The four kids skipped down the beach. When they were far ahead of Mimi and Papa, they dropped down onto the sand.

"Is Ranger Burnside following us?" asked Grant, picking sand out of an oyster shell. "Maybe she lives in the dunes and she just doesn't want a bunch of kids bothering her."

"I wouldn't bother her," said Quincy. He scooped up a pile of sand with his scallop shell.

"Do you think Ranger Burnside was digging in the dunes behind the lighthouse?" asked Amelia.

"It was so dark. It could have been her," said Christina. "The person was tall and wearing pants. She fits that description. All I know is someone is definitely trying to scare us away from the dunes. But I don't understand why."

Grant leaned over and whispered, "Why does that lady behind you keep staring at us?"

Christina peeked over her shoulder. Sitting in a yellow and white striped sand chair and wearing a wide-brimmed blue hat was the lady who wanted to buy Ben and Arabella's house.

"That's Mrs. Gage," Amelia whispered.
"I thought so," Christina said.

The kids huddled closely to talk. Mrs. Gage inspected the foursome one last time, perched her sunglasses on her nose, picked up her chair, and sauntered away.

Just then, a mighty gust of wind grabbed her hat. She dropped her chair and chased the bouncing hat down the beach.

"The storm will be here before the day is over," said Christina. "We have to solve this mystery fast. And we're going to have to go back to the lighthouse to do it!"

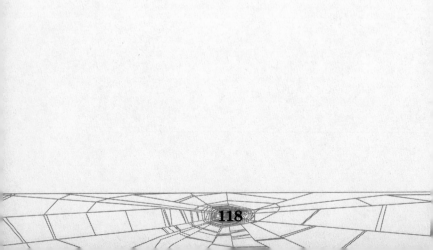

20
DUNE SHACK SAND

The wind on Cape Cod was picking up and the waves were rising higher and higher. Dark clouds rumbled across the sky. Waves crashed. Seagulls squawked. The storm was fast approaching.

"Mimi, we're going to Mrs. Winthrop's lighthouse to check it out before the storm comes," said Christina to her grandma.

"OK," said Mimi reluctantly, "but promise me you'll come straight back to Arabella's cottage as soon as you finish. This storm is due to make landfall late in the day."

"We'll hurry, Mimi," Christina promised.

Amelia grabbed Quincy's hand and the kids tore down the beach as fast as their legs would carry them. The beach was starting to clear out except for a few storm-watchers. A few seagulls drifted along the shore and large, long-legged cranes picked through seashells. But for the most part, even the birds were heading for safety.

"Wow, look at those waves!" yelled Grant. "I've never seen waves that big except on The Weather Channel."

When they got to Nauset Lighthouse, Amelia tried to open the heavy, black door. It was locked. "Mother must have already left," she said.

"Let's take a look at the dune our friend was digging on," said Christina.

They sprinted around the back of the lighthouse to the dunes where the shadowy figure had worked.

"Wow, he—or she—really dug a lot of sand off this dune," said Amelia. "Look at all the holes." Amelia brushed her hair from her face as sand swirled around the dune.

"You probably won't be able to tell someone was ever here once this storm comes through," said Christina. "It's going to blow the sand so much that no one will notice."

"Except us," said Quincy.

"There's got to be more than potholes in the dune," said Christina.

The dune grasses waved wildly as the kids roamed in between each hill of sand searching for something. They didn't know what.

Then they saw it. Tucked into one sand dune and surrounded by several more stood a rickety, wooden dune shack. Wispy dune grass camouflaged its roof. A rusty padlock held the door closed.

"It's a dune shack," said Grant. "I knew old Burnside was a dune dweller!"

Christina jiggled the padlock. "It's locked," she said. "But we can probably see between these slats of wood." She bent down and peered between two splintered boards.

"Too dark. I wish I had my flashlight," said Christina.

Quincy whipped one out of his pocket. "I never leave home without it," he quipped, handing it to her.

Christina stuffed the flashlight between a gap in the slats and peered through. Inside, a red wheelbarrow half filled with sand stood in the middle of the tiny shack. Several shovels leaned against one wall next to a couple of cardboard boxes. Scattered everywhere were sky-blue plastic bags with orange labels. Some looked as if they were full of something. Others lay empty in stacks.

"I can't make out what the labels on the bags say," said Christina, squinting through the cracks.

"They look like the bags of sand that Mom and Dad buy for our sandbox," said Grant.

"Someone is stealing sand and bagging it!" said Christina, incredulous.

"You're not supposed to dig up the sand in our dunes and sell it!!" cried Amelia, outraged.

Christina's phone beeped. "Where r u?" texted Mimi.

"It's Mimi," Christina said. "We better get back home FAST!"

"Almost there," Christina typed as she ran. By the time she hit SEND, the kids were sprinting across the field in front of the Three Sisters. The first band of icy rain from the storm pelted their faces.

21

LANDFALL!

"The nor'easter is expected to make landfall somewhere between Boston and Provincetown, Massachusetts," said the television news anchor. The kids were glued to the TV in Arabella and Ben's kitchen. "Residents can expect the storm to bring freezing rain and possibly snow to parts of Massachusetts and New York."

"It might snooooow!" yelled Grant, jumping up and down. He and Christina saw very little of the white stuff at their home in Georgia.

The anchor continued, "All areas along the Atlantic Coast from Maine to North Carolina can expect oversized waves that can cause beach erosion and structural damage. This is especially true for Cape Cod, Martha's Vineyard, and Nantucket."

"That's us!" screamed Quincy, clapping his hands.

"Wind gusts associated with these storms can exceed hurricane force in intensity. Now let's turn it over to Brianna Brown, reporting live from Race Point Beach."

"I've got some hot chocolate for you," said Arabella. She poured steaming chocolate into four mugs and stuck a peppermint swizzle stick in each.

"I'm glad you're back," said Mimi, as she sat down at the kitchen table. "How was the lighthouse?"

"Mrs. Winthrop had already left so we came home," said Christina. Her brown hair stuck out in all directions as she pulled off her lime green knit cap.

"Did you kids happen to see Ben?" Arabella asked. "He went to the grocery store to get some extra things just in case this storm is worse than we expect it to be."

"Do you think it's NOT going to be bad?" asked Grant, looking disappointed.

"Well, a bad nor'easter can bring us about three feet of snow. We're not expecting that! Thank goodness!" said Arabella.

"Do you mind if we take our hot chocolate to the porch, Mimi?" asked Christina.

"It's fine with me," said Mimi, "if Arabella doesn't mind. Just stay bundled up. Papa is taking a nap and I have a few emails to answer. I'll be in our room if you need me."

"I brought in the chairs, but you're welcome to go to the porch," Arabella remarked. "Here are some sandwiches to go along with the hot chocolate." She handed Christina a plate piled high with peanut butter and jelly sandwiches.

The kids each grabbed a sandwich from the plate. They plopped down on the porch floor to watch the gusts of wind and rain.

"This is cool," said Grant.

"Happens all the time," said Amelia.

Christina licked a dribble of grape jelly from the edge of her sandwich and took a bite. Our clues just aren't getting me anywhere, she thought. I don't know where to go next.

She wiped her mouth with a napkin and said, "We're pretty sure someone is stealing sand and selling it. Now we just have to figure out who. Let's make a list."

"It's got to be Ranger Burnside," said Grant. "There's no other reason she wouldn't like us. We're a bunch of great kids!"

"Right!" said Quincy. He and Grant giggled.

"But what about that Mrs. Cage? She was listening to every word we said on the beach," said Grant. "I was watching her."

"Do you think she is scaring us because she wants to buy our house, too?" asked Amelia.

Grant shrugged his shoulders. Quincy's lip quivered at the thought of moving from his home.

"OK, Ranger Burnside is the number one suspect," said Christina, typing, "#1

Burnside" on a To Do List application on her cell phone. "Next, there is Mrs. Gage." She added "#2 Gage."

"I think Mrs. Cage is just nosey," said Grant. "Or maybe she's cagey. Get it? Cage? Cagey?" Quincy was the only one to laugh at Grant's joke.

"It's Mrs. Gage, not cage," said Christina to Grant.

"Or it could be someone we don't know," said Amelia.

"Well, they sure do know us!" Christina said, typing #3 and a question mark.

The four sat in silence, sipping hot chocolate and watching the rain fall in icy sheets around the cottage.

Christina jumped to her feet. "I can't sit here doing nothing. Let's go down to the beach and watch the waves," she said. "Do you have some rain gear, Amelia?"

"Lots!" said Amelia.

"We're going to Amelia's house," called Christina to Arabella. Arabella waved and the kids bounded off to the house next door.

Within minutes, they scampered out of the Winthrop's home outfitted with shiny black rubber boots and bright yellow slickers over their heavy winter clothes. As they raced down the wooden walkway between the two houses, Christina noticed a trail of wet, sandy footprints.

Suddenly, Grant yelled, "Stop!" He reached down and picked up a torn piece of blue and orange paper stuck in the bushes alongside Arabella's house.

"Oh my gosh!" Grant said, waving the paper wildly. "This is a piece of the sandbags my parents buy for our sandbox! 'ABC Sandbox Sand,'" he read from the label. "This is it! This is it! It's the label from the bags we saw in the dune shack. These are the same ones we buy at home!"

22
THE ABC'S OF SAND

Christina snatched the piece of bag from Grant's hand and stared at it in disbelief.

"Why is this label so close to your house?" Christina asked Amelia. Her mind was spinning nearly as fast as the wind was blowing.

"It could have blown here," cried Amelia, as the wind whipped between the two cottages.

"I saw sandy footprints back there right before Grant saw the piece of bag," said Christina, retracing her steps. The kids followed her. They searched for the prints as sand from the nearby dunes peppered them.

"There they are!" said Christina. "Sand has almost covered them up. But you can still see one."

"I'm scared," said Amelia. "This person knows right where we live."

All four kids looked over their shoulders.

"There's no way anyone is out in this stuff," yelled Grant, cinching the drawstring around his hood.

"Except crazy us!" Quincy called back.

Another hefty gust of wind tore between the two houses, nearly knocking Quincy down. Putting her back to the wind, Christina lifted her rain slicker and shoved the sandbag label into her jacket pocket where it would be safe. Turning back around, she shouted, "Let's get away from here!"

Arm in arm, the kids braced against the driving wind and trudged past the safety of their two houses toward the dunes and the beach.

By now, the raging winds were doing serious damage. "Watch out!" screamed Christina as a small metal sign flew over their heads like a missile. That's kind of funny, she thought. The sign said NO WALKING ON THE DUNES!

"Look!" yelled Grant, pointing to a car half covered by sand.

The kids trudged through puddles of rain and salty seawater blowing from the ocean.

Christina's head was beginning to hurt from the roar of the wind in her ears. Why am I going out here, she thought. What do I expect to find?

"Mother's going to kill us!" yelled Quincy, staggering between Grant and Amelia with his head bent down.

When they got to the dunes, the roar became even louder as gigantic waves pounded the Cape Cod coast. "My ears are throbbing!" screamed Amelia.

The kids trudged between the maze of massive dunes, making their way to the beach.

Tall, thin blades of dune grass waved wildly, swiping at their faces. The force of the wind bent small trees and bushes nearly to the ground. Sand swirled and stung their eyes.

The kids rounded the edge of a dune to find themselves in a small area surrounded by towering dunes and somewhat sheltered from the wind. They froze in their tracks.

It was the back of a man—wearing a shiny black rain slicker and hat. They watched, motionless, as he slammed a red-handled shovel deep into the sand. A stack of empty blue and orange bags anchored by a huge rock sat at his feet. At least ten bags full of sand leaned up against the dunes.

"Ben!!" screamed Quincy, running toward his friend.

Ben slowly turned around. "What are you kids doing out here in this weather?" he yelled gruffly. "You could get hurt."

"What are you doing here?" asked Christina.

"You were so worried about the sand that I came out to see what I could find," Ben replied. "I just discovered this work area. It looks like someone is stealing sand."

Christina pulled up her slicker, stuck her hand into the pocket of her blue fleece jacket, and fished out the note: TONIGHT—100 bags of sand. "This was a note you wrote to yourself, isn't it, Ben?" Christina asked. "It fell out of your car and Grant stepped on it." She held the note out for him to see.

"And we found a piece of these bags in the bushes beside your house," added Christina. "ABC Sandbox Sand stands for Arabella and Ben Cawthorne, doesn't it? You've been trying to scare us away from the dunes so we wouldn't discover that you are bagging the sand!"

Ben threw down his shovel, grabbed Quincy's hand, and moved toward the kids. He towered over them. A huge gust of wind swirled through the dunes, dusting their faces with fine granules of sand.

Amelia began to cry.

Ben dropped to his knees. "I'm sorry," he said, covering his face with his hands.

Just then, Ranger Anna Burnside and two park officials appeared from around a dune.

"We're going to have to arrest you, Mr. Cawthorne," said Ranger Burnside. "This is National Park Service property. It's against the law to take sand from the dunes and sell it for a profit."

Seconds later, Mimi, Papa, and Mrs. Winthrop appeared. "I've been texting you," said Mimi. "What is going on here?"

Christina threw her arms around her grandma. She suddenly realized that the nor'easter rain had turned into flakes of snow and the water running down her cheeks was tears, just like Amelia's.

23
SAND, SNOW, AND SUN

Christina, Grant, Mimi, and Papa sat quietly on the porch of Arabella and Ben's cottage. They watched the snow drift down in a shower of white.

"I think the storm is passing by," said Papa, pointing to a small patch of blue sky in the distance.

Mrs. Winthrop appeared with Quincy and Arabella. All had red eyes and tear-streaked faces. "We want to say goodbye to Ben," Amelia said, a quiver in her voice.

The group was silent as Ben, Arabella, and Anna Burnside walked out onto the porch.

"I did a bad thing," Ben said to everybody. "No one should ever harm the dunes for any reason." He leaned down to Amelia and Quincy. "Don't worry, you two. I will be all right. I've learned my lesson. And when I come back home, I'll make this up to you."

Then he turned to Christina and Grant. "You two are good detectives and good friends."

He walked down the steps with Ranger Burnside, who turned around and nodded to Christina.

Mimi wrapped her arms around Arabella. "He is a good person, Arabella," Mimi said. "He merely lost his way for a while."

"We'll get through this," Arabella replied. "Just this afternoon, Mrs. Gage called and suggested we turn the cottage into a bed and breakfast since we didn't want to sell it. I think we should. It will help us get on our feet, and I know Ben will get back to fishing some day. He's a fisherman at heart."

Arabella stepped back into the cottage, followed by Mrs. Winthrop.

"Maybe we should take a little walk through the snow before it melts," said Papa.

Mimi and Christina headed down the steps into the crisp white snow. "You are a good detective, Christina," Mimi said, zipping up her red fleece jacket. "I don't know where you get it!" They laughed.

"Remember when we saw the whale this morning?" said Christina. "I knew it was a sign that everything was going to turn out OK. I just wasn't sure how it was going to happen."

"Everything always turns out OK, Christina," Mimi reminded her, "as long as we keep searching for the truth."

WHACK! A miniature snowball smacked Christina's arm.

"Hey! Is there snow on the dunes?" yelled Grant, galloping toward the beach with Quincy close behind. "Can you dune ski? I want to dune ski!!"

"No playing on the dunes!" Christina yelled back and laughed.

A shimmering Cape Cod sun suddenly broke through the clouds. "Come on," Christina called to Amelia. "Gotta keep up with those boys!"

Hand in hand, the two friends sprinted toward the sparkling blue ocean. "Last one in is a rotten clam!" Christina shouted.

Well, that was fun!

Wow, glad we solved that mystery!

Where shall we go next?

EVERYWHERE!

The End

Now...go to

www.carolemarshmysteries.com
and...

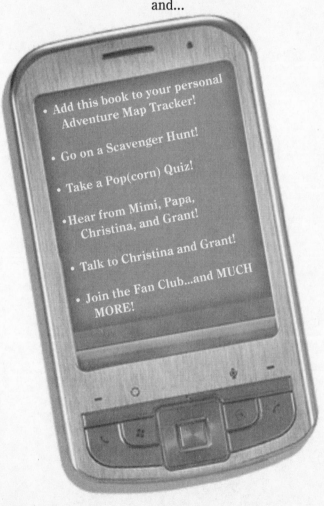

- Add this book to your personal Adventure Map Tracker!

- Go on a Scavenger Hunt!

- Take a Pop(corn) Quiz!

- Hear from Mimi, Papa, Christina, and Grant!

- Talk to Christina and Grant!

- Join the Fan Club...and MUCH MORE!

GLOSSARY

concoction: a mixture of various ingredients or elements

engrossed: having all of one's attention absorbed by someone or something

erosion: the process of eroding, or gradually wearing away, by wind, water, or other natural agents

habitat: the natural home or environment of an animal, plant, or other organism

impermeable: not allowing fluid to pass through

incredulous: unwilling or unable to believe something

maneuver: a movement or series of moves requiring skill and care

mollusk: an invertebrate of a large phylum that includes snails, slugs, mussels, and octopuses

SAT GLOSSARY

crustacean: pertaining to a division of arthropods, containing lobsters, crabs, crawfish, etc.

disobedient: neglecting or refusing to obey

illuminate: to supply with light

skiff: a small, light boat propelled by oars

submerge: to place or plunge under water

Enjoy this exciting excerpt from:

THE MYSTERY

AT

Fort
Sumter

Highway 17, South Carolina

CHRISTINA yawned. It seemed so very strange. She and her brother Grant usually traveled with their grandparents to Charleston in the spring or summer. Yet here they were, barreling down a dark, wet, sleet-slick highway in the dead of winter.

They had left Mimi and Papa's Gullah blue-doored home in Savannah's historic district just awhile ago. Papa's big gray SUV had sailed over the Talmadge Bridge and across the South Carolina state line. There was no one on the dark and mysterious road. The sleet-laden trees hung low over the highway. It looked like they were driving through a dark, lacy tunnel. The full moon only now and then peeked down through the leaves like a big white eyeball spying on them.

Papa drove fast, but watched carefully for the **enormous** alligators that were known to cross the highway at night. The thought made Christina shiver. She snugged further down into the Clemson afghan Papa had tossed back to her when she complained she was freezing. Across the seat, Grant hunkered over his video game, the greenish light from the monitor creating a skeletal glow in the car. Mimi was asleep.

They stopped at Green Pond to go to the bathroom. In the old store, Christina marveled at the array of enormous cooking pots and ladles large enough to hold a head. She wondered what kind of creatures you could catch in these lowcountry waters that would require such tools. Again, she shivered.

As they sped on toward Charleston, Christina read the curious sign names by moonlight: Ashepoo...Combahee...Edisto... Pon Pon Plantation. Gray beards of Spanish moss swung from trees and even street signs. Ghostly shadows flickered on the road. It reminded Christina that Charleston was known as the Most Haunted City in America.

Usually that would be good news. Usually, they would be headed to Charleston in spring during the garden season when the

Spoleto arts festival was going on, or in summer to visit the beaches at Folly or Wild Dunes. Mimi would be working on a new kids' mystery book, and she and Grant would be helping her. But this night they were not headed for sun and fun—they were headed to a funeral. Mimi's Aunt Lulu had died.

To make things worse, it was the Christmas holidays. They'd been visiting with their grandparents when the call came, which is why they happened to be cooped up in this cold car all glum and sad. So what kind of fun could this be? What kind of mystery adventure? What kind of Christmas?

Christina didn't even want to think about it. Of course, there was no way she could possibly know that it would turn out to be what she would later describe as "the worst one of all"...what Grant later called "the best one of all!"

Papa made a swooping right turn and they faced a city glittering in the foggy cold. "Charleston," he announced.

Christina glanced at the car's digital clock: MIDNIGHT.

"Of course it is," she groaned, and hid beneath the afghan as the car bumped down an ancient cobblestone street into town.

1

"WHAT FORT IS THIS?"

GRANT yawned. When the car stopped, he looked up to see that they were parked in front of what looked like a grand fortress.

"Are we going to sleep at Fort Sumter?" he asked, yawning again. He turned off his video player, thrusting the car from green gloom to just plain old black gloom.

"This is not Fort Sumter," said Papa, stretching, his cowboy hat scraping the roof.

"This is a hotel. It's the old Citadel building, and yes, the young men who once stayed here would say it is indeed a fortress." Papa laughed.

From the back seat, Christina and Grant stared at the edifice shrouded in fogged light, then stared at each other. They shrugged their shoulders.

"Looks like a fort to me," Christina whispered to her brother.

"Towers...turrets...gun ports..." said Grant. "Yep, looks like a fort to me."

A GIANT yawn escaped from the front seat. "Are we sleeping at Fort Sumter?!" cried Mimi.

She stretched and sat straight up, her short blond hair a spiky mess.

"Oh, for gosh sakes!" moaned Papa. "It's a hotel! Or, we can sleep in the car."

"Uh, no thanks!" said Christina, shoving the Clemson afghan aside. She gathered her things. "There is no bathroom in the car."

"Or television," reminded Grant, eagerly grabbing his backpack.

Papa opened the car door as a sleepy bellman in a uniform approached. "No TV. It's late. It's bedtime. Let's go, pard'ners—NOW!"

The kids, and even Mimi, "hopped to."

"Wow," Christina whispered to her brother. "Papa sounds like a drill sergeant or something."

"He's just tired," said Mimi. "That drive in the sleet on the dark road is nerve-wracking."

"Mimi!" said Grant. "You were asleep...how do you know?"

Mimi turned around. Her eyes were still red from weeping over poor Aunt Lulu. "Now, Grant, you know how I have eyes in the back of my head?"

"Yes, ma'am," Grant said.

"Well, guess what?" said Mimi. "I can also 'backseat drive' your Papa from the front seat—even with my eyes closed."

Papa, who was holding her door open, shook his head. "It's true, Grant, and don't forget it. You can't get anything past Mimi." He gave Mimi a weary wink.

Mimi smiled and perked up. She hopped out of the car and followed the bellman and their luggage cart inside. Papa, Christina, and Grant followed obediently.

"Well, do we even get dinner?" Grant asked forlornly. He rubbed his tummy and tried to look like a starving waif. He and his sister waited eagerly for the answer.

Mimi and Papa barely turned their heads around, but together they said, "NO!"

As Christina entered the spooky, fortlike hotel, she noted the time on the lobby clock.

"Forgetaboutit, Grant," she said sadly, putting her arm around her brother's shoulders. "It's closer to breakfast than dinnertime. I have some M&Ms in my backpack. We'll make do."

"Great!" grumbled Grant. "Next, I guess we'll find out we're staying in the dungeon?"

Papa hovered over the check-in desk. A skeletal-looking desk clerk handed him a key. "The room you requested, sir," they overheard him say. "The Dungeon Suite."

Christina and Grant exchanged shocked glances, and nervously followed their grandparents into the gloom of the darkened lobby.

2
TO THE DUNGEON

As they made their way through the spooky lobby and onto an elevator, Christina spied strange shadows dancing on the walls...or was that just from the candlelight? Tinkling water made her think of a drippy, old dungeon, but when the elevator doors opened, they found themselves in a regular hotel corridor. The bellman shoved the cart ahead of them and stopped at a door at the end of the hall.

"Room 13," muttered Grant. "Naturally."

Inside, the kids were happy to see that it was a two-room suite, so they had a sofa bed to pull out and their own television, and the fridge and microwave were in their room. Soon, and in silence, they had all gotten into their pajamas. Papa mumbled something that sounded like "Gunnite" and headed to bed. Mimi helped the kids manage the sofa bed, then curled up with them against a bank of pillows.

"So what happens next, Mimi?" Christina asked her grandmother, who still looked very sad.

"Not sure," said Mimi. "I haven't heard from Aunt Lulu in years. I only got one quick phone call about her death, from a stranger, so I don't really even know where to find her!"

Grant's eyes opened very, very wide. "So you mean we're going to have to search Charleston for a dead body?!" He scrunched down into the blankets.

"Grant!" squealed his sister.

"It's ok," Mimi assured him. "I am sad, but Lulu was very old. All her family died long ago, so that's one reason she was always so hard to stay in touch with. She really isn't even my aunt. I, uh, I think she's the aunt of my mother's third cousin once removed."

Christina and Grant stared at one another, then burst into laughter.

Now Mimi was offended. "And just what's so funny?"

"Sorrrry," sputtered Christina, and she and Grant burst into laughter yet again.

Mimi frowned, then laughed herself. "I know, I know," she said. "It sounds strange. But really, I had to come."

"For the funeral?" Christina offered somberly. She punched her brother to stop his uncontrollable giggling, especially since he was slobbering on her side of the covers.

"No," said Mimi, matter-of-factly. "There is no funeral. Lulu was cremated."

"Then...?" Christina prodded.

Mimi sighed. "I had to come for the reading of the will. It seems that my name is mentioned."

"JACKPOT!" cried Grant, giving a high-five sign to his sister.